LUNCH ON
PIRATE SH

For Hadley xx – CH

For Wilf and Rafe Hodges, with love – KS

SIMON & SCHUSTER
First published in Great Britain in 2018 by Simon & Schuster UK Ltd
1st Floor, 222 Gray's Inn Road, London, WC1X 8HB • A CBS Company
Text copyright © 2018 Caryl Hart • Illustrations copyright © 2018 Kristina Stephenson
The right of Caryl Hart and Kristina Stephenson to be identified as the author and
illustrator of this work has been asserted by them in accordance with the Copyright,
Designs and Patents Act, 1988 • All rights reserved, including the right of reproduction in
whole or in part in any form • A CIP catalogue record for this book is available from
the British Library upon request.
978-0-8570-7942-8 (PB) • 978-1-4711-1843-2 (eBook)
Printed in China • 10 9 8 7 6 5 4 3 2 1

LUNCH ON A PIRATE SHIP

Caryl Hart and Kristina Stephenson

SIMON & SCHUSTER

London   New York   Sydney   Toronto   New Delhi

One fine day, a little boy called Jack
Was playing with his toys in his yard, out back.
It was so much fun being out and about
That he didn't even hear his mum call out . . .

"**Lunch is ready!**"
little Jack's mum cried.

But when at last, Jack came inside
He couldn't bear to eat his lunch,
Because . . .

... his chips were cold and his baked beans crunched!

"I can't eat this soggy old chip
I'd rather have lunch on a pirate ship!
I'll sail with the crew far out to sea,
They're bound to have lunch for a boy like me."

So he . . .

. . . SKIPPED

and he

TRIPPED

to the bustling docks

And there was a pirate ship, tied to the rocks.

"Ahoy there, lad," the pirates cried,
"Climb on board if you'd like a ride!"

"I've come for lunch," said brave young Jack,
"I'd like to have a taste of a pirate snack."
"Of course!" grinned the pirates,
"Try this dish. It's . . .

. . . pickled crabs and rotten fish."

"Rotten fish? Oh yuck!" Jack said.
"One bite of THAT and we'll drop down dead!"
"Arrr!" said the captain, "Whatever shall we do?
We need a big lunch for a pirate crew!"

So they . . .

... SPLASHED and they DASHED

through a thousand waves

To a land where giants live in deep, dark caves.

"Oi!" growled a giant. "Hey! Who goes there?
Enter very carefully – if you dare!"

The pirates inched closer, "It's only us!" they cried.
"We're here for some lunch please. Can we come inside?"
"All right," grinned the giant, "you're just in time.
Have a lovely jubbly bowl full of . . .

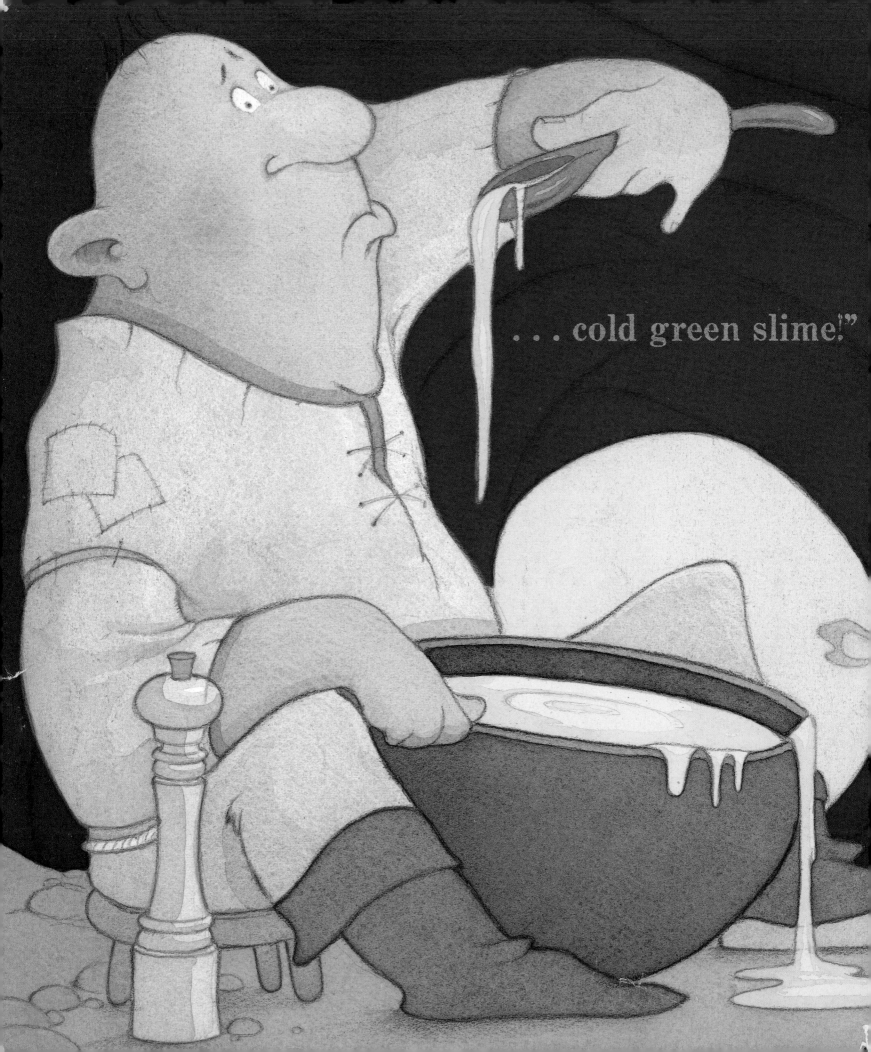

"Cold green slime?" groaned Jack. "No way!
If we ate that gloop we'd be poorly all day."

"You're right," sighed the giant,
"We need a tasty treat. I rather think
a picnic would be very hard to beat."

Then Jack sniffed . . .

. . . a sweet aroma, drifting through the wood.

He spied a wisp of purple smoke that **DID** smell good.

So they all jumped up on the giant's huge back

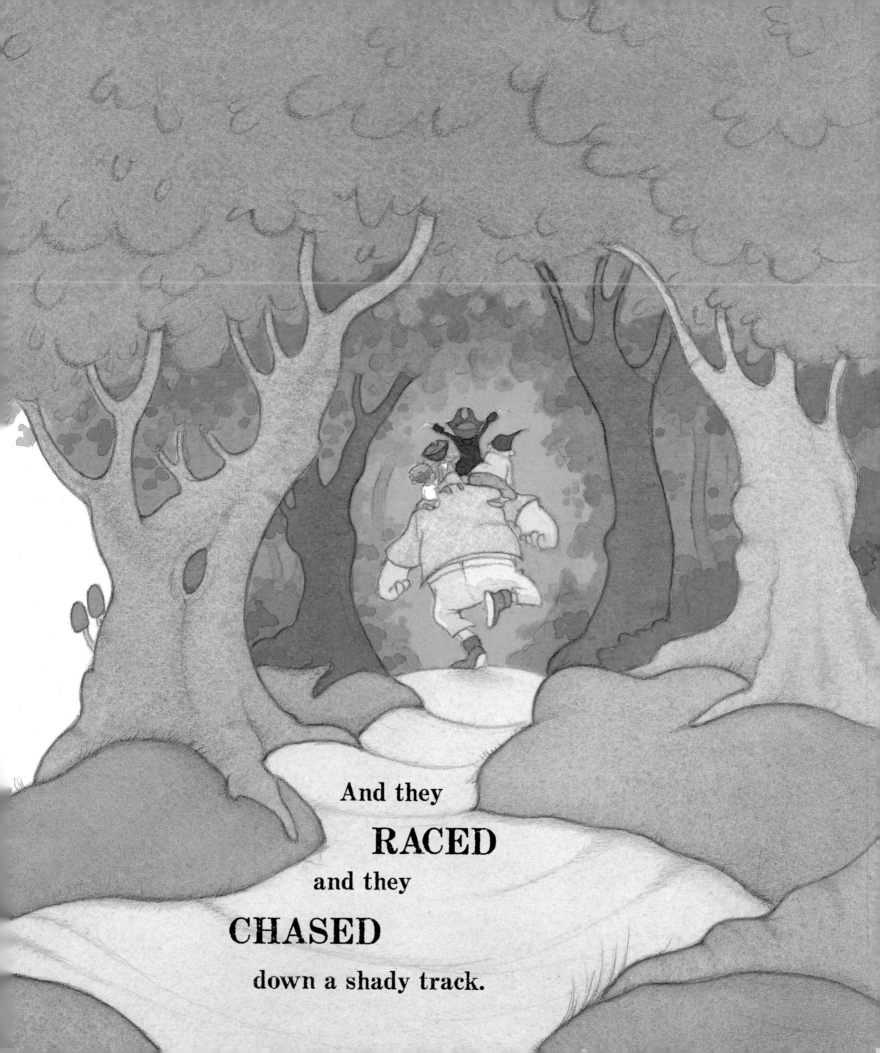

And they
RACED
and they
CHASED
down a shady track.

There in a field by a bubbling stream
Was a table filled with cupcakes,
cherries and ice cream.

"Hooray!" cried Jack,

"THIS lovely feast will do
For a giant and a boy
and a pirate crew."

So they . . .

...TRIPPED

and they

TRAPPED

across a creaking bridge.

There was pie in the oven
and jelly in the fridge.

But a hungry troll had tricked them,
it jumped up! **BOO!**

"The tasty treat today,
my friends, is . . .

. . . ALL OF YOU!"

"HELP!" cried the giant
as he splashed across the stream.

"HELP!" cried the pirates,
dropping their ice cream.

"HELP!" yelled Jack
as they dashed along the track.
They sprinted from the hungry
troll and didn't look back!

They DASHED and they CRASHED past the deep, dark caves.

They BUNDLED and they TUMBLED in their ship across the waves.

They SPRINTED up to Jack's house,
as quick as quick can be . . .

"Ah, THERE you are," said Jack's mum,
"You're just in time for tea!

There's . . .

Piping hot spaghetti topped with melted cheese.
There's crunchy munchy carrots, and teeny tiny peas.

There's sticky apple doughnuts
if you eat your greens,
And bowls of juicy strawberries
with freshly whipped cream."

They ate and they ate
and they ate lots more,

Then the giant cleared the plates, while the pirates swept the floor.

"You know," said Jack as they all sat down to rest,

"Eating out is QUITE exciting . . .

. . . but Mum's cooking tastes the **best!**"